RICKY ZOOM
Welcome to Wheelford

By Annie Auerbach

This book is based on the Property Ricky Zoom © Frog Box / Entertainment One UK Limited 2020

All rights reserved. Published by Scholastic Inc., *Publishers since 1920*. SCHOLASTIC and associated logos are trademarks and/or registered trademarks of Scholastic Inc.

The publisher does not have any control over and does not assume any responsibility for author or third-party websites or their content.

No part of this publication may be reproduced, stored in a retrieval system, or transmitted in any form or by any means, electronic, mechanical, photocopying, recording, or otherwise, without written permission of the publisher. For information regarding permission, write to Scholastic Inc., Attention: Permissions Department, 557 Broadway, New York, NY 10012.

This book is a work of fiction. Names, characters, places, and incidents are either the product of the author's imagination or are used fictitiously, and any resemblance to actual persons, living or dead, business establishments, events, or locales is entirely coincidental.

ISBN 978-1-338-67741-6

10 9 8 7 6 5 4 3 2 1   20 21 22 23 24

Printed in the U.S.A.   40

First printing 2020

SCHOLASTIC INC.

MEET
RICKY ZOOM

"Speed spoiler visor"

Ricky Zoom is a rescue bike who likes to go fast! He is the confident leader of the Bike Buddies and his favorite things to do are rev his engines and zoom around Wheelford.

"Let's zoom out!"

FUN FACT:
Ricky has a visor that helps him with speed and distance. It also has night vision!

MEET
HANK AND
HELEN ZOOM

Helen and Hank Zoom are Wheelford's leading rescue bikes. Daring and brave, they are always the first to respond to emergencies in the town.

FUN FACT:
Helen works as an ambulance driver and Hank is involved with the fire rescue.

MEET LOOP

"Leave it to Loop!"

Loop Hoopla is a dirt bike who just wants to have fun—like doing loop de loops and jumping ramps.

"Loopy boosters go!"

FUN FACT:
Loop's boosters power up his stunts.

MEET SCOOTIO

"ZoomCam go!"

Scootio Whizzbang calls herself a "gadget guru." She's a scooter whose technical genius matches her can-do attitude.

"Scootbops go!"

FUN FACT:
Scootio has six little robot creatures at her command called Scootbops!

MEET DJ

"Revvv on!"

DJ Rumbler is a green trike with a heart of gold. His tools all fit on his robotic arm, making him a handy pal to have around.

"Activating toolbox!"

FUN FACT:
There's nothing DJ can't build—or knock down!

MEET TOOT

Toot is Ricky's younger sister. Toot may be smaller than the other bikes, but she's got a *big* personality!

"Time to roll!"

FUN FACT:
Toot loves to tell embarrassing stories about her brother, Ricky!

THE BIKE BUDDIES

Ricky, Scootio, DJ, and Loop make up the Bike Buddies.

Together, the friends support each other in each adventure. According to the Bike Buddies, friendship is number one!

FUN FACT:
Each bike brings something different to a challenge. When the Bike Buddies work together, they can overcome anything!

MEET STEEL AWESOME

Steel Awesome loves to perform amazing stunts! He's a movie star and comic book hero all in one. Some of his biggest fans are Ricky and the Bike Buddies.

FUN FACT:
Since he's a celebrity, Steel Awesome has packs of adoring fans—including himself!

MEET
MRS. BIKELY

Mrs. Bikely is a supportive teacher whose spirited and fun lessons help the Buddies develop their goals, imagination, and independence.

FUN FACT:
She has a not-so-secret crush on Steel Awesome!

MEET
MAXWELL

Maxwell is the town mechanic. Whatever a bike needs, Maxwell will help with a smile and a story about the good ol' days.

FUN FACT:
Maxwell is a good-natured bike who has been everywhere and seen everything.

MEET DASHER

Dasher is Ricky's cousin. He loves racing and doing stunts. It must run in the family!

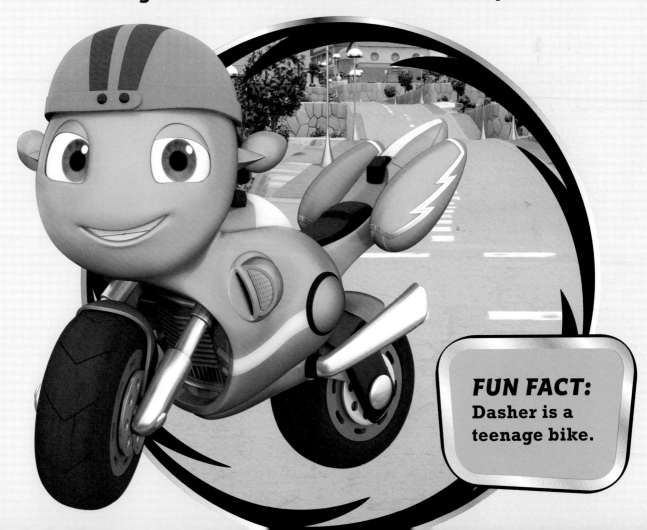

FUN FACT: Dasher is a teenage bike.

RICKY'S HOUSE

Ricky's house has a wonderful view of Wheelford and doubles as the rescue headquarters for the town.

Here, emergencies come up on a big map. Then Helen and Hank use their "gear up" stations to respond to them. When they are ready, ramps on the outside of the house give the rescue duo a quick and easy route into town.

FUN FACT:
There's a rescue pod
at the top of the house!

MAXWELL'S SERVICE STATION

Maxwell runs the Service Station in Wheelford.

Maxwell's Service Station has everything a bike needs. On the outside, there is a drive-through bike wash and spray tower. Inside, there are gadgets, tools, and a large service lift where Maxwell can use his robotic arms to repair any mechanical problem.

THE ADVENTURE PARK

Full of ramps, loop de loops, and tracks to race around, the Adventure Park is the most fun a bike can have on two wheels!

FUN FACT:
Steel Awesome often performs stunts at the Adventure Park.

WHEELFORD ELEMENTARY SCHOOL

Ricky and the Bike Buddies attend Wheelford Elementary School. Here, they learn lots of life lessons, including what makes a good role model. And they have lots of fun, too! For gym class in school, they play Motoball.

FUN FACT:
There is a racetrack that runs along the top of the school!

Wheelford is an amazing place to live—especially if you've got two wheels.

Every day brings zoomtastic races, rescues, and adventures!

RICKY

HELEN AND HANK

TOOT

DJ

SCOOTIO

LOOP

Ricky Zoom © Frog Box/Ent. One UK Ltd. 2020.

Ricky Zoom © Frog Box/Ent. One UK Ltd. 2020.

Ricky Zoom © Frog Box/Ent. One UK Ltd. 2020.

TOOT

Toot is Ricky's younger sister. She's sweet, sassy, and eager for adventure. Toot may be smaller than the other bikes, but she's got a big personality!

HELEN AND HANK

Helen and Hank Zoom are Wheelford's leading rescue bikes and Ricky and Toot's parents. Daring and brave, they are always the first to respond to emergencies in the town.

RICKY

Ricky Zoom is a rescue bike who likes to go fast! He is the confident leader of the Bike Buddies and his favorite things to do are rev his engines and zoom around Wheelford.

LOOP

Loop is a dirt bike who just wants to have fun—like doing loop de loops and jumping ramps. He is wide-eyed and adventurous, but sometimes gets distracted.

SCOOTIO

Scootio calls herself a "gadget guru." She's a scooter whose technical genius matches her can-do attitude. She is always eager to try out a new solution to a problem.

DJ

DJ is a green trike with a heart of gold. His super toolbox trunk is filled with everything from wrenches to hooks to hammers. They all fit on his robotic arm, making him a handy pal to have around.

Scholastic Inc., 557 Broadway, New York, NY 10012
Made in Jefferson City, USA